HI! FLY GUY

LEVEL 2
DEVELOPING READER
250-750 WORDS

Tedd Arnold

P9-ELR-982

Cartwheel BOOKS®

SCHOLASTIC INC.
New York   Toronto   London   Auckland   Sydney
Mexico City   New Delhi   Hong Kong   Buenos Aires

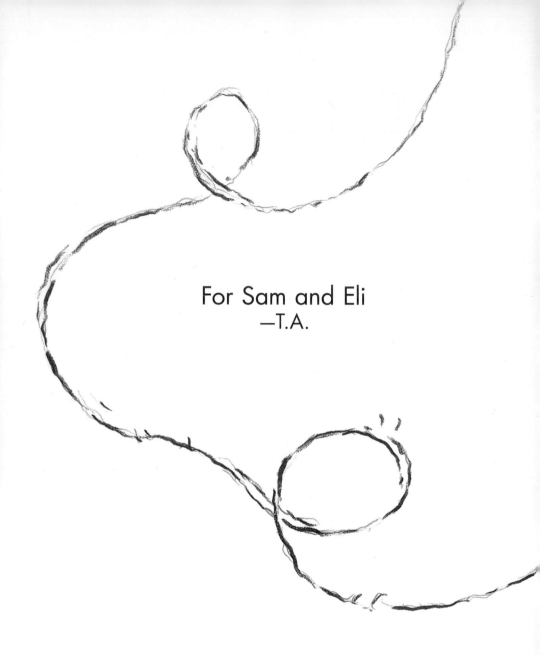

For Sam and Eli
—T.A.

Copyright © 2005 by Tedd Arnold.

All rights reserved. Published by Scholastic Inc.
SCHOLASTIC, CARTWHEEL BOOKS, and associated logos
are trademarks and/or registered trademarks of Scholastic Inc.
Lexile is a registered trademark of MetaMetrics, Inc.

Library of Congress Cataloging-in-Publication Data is available.

ISBN-13: 978-0-439-85311-8
ISBN-10: 0-439-85311-7

41 40   40   18 19/0

Printed in the U.S.A.
This edition first printing, May 2009

Chapter 1

A fly went flying.

He was looking
for something to eat—

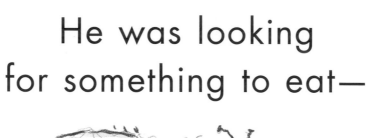

something tasty,

something slimy.

A boy went walking.

He was looking for
something to catch—
something smart,
something for
The Amazing Pet Show.

They met.

The boy caught the fly
in a jar.
"A pet!" he said.

The fly was mad.
He wanted to be free.
He stomped his foot
and said— **BUZZ!**

The boy was surprised.
He said, "You know my name!
You are the smartest pet in
the world!"

Chapter 2

Buzz took the fly home.

"This is my pet," Buzz said to Mom and Dad.

"He is smart. He can say
my name. Listen!"

Buzz opened the jar.
The fly flew out.

"Flies can't be pets!" said
Dad. "They are pests!"
He got the fly swatter.
The fly cried— **BUZZ!**

And Buzz came to the rescue.
"You are right," said Dad.
"This fly <u>is</u> smart!"

"He needs a name," said Mom.
Buzz thought for a minute.
"Fly Guy," said Buzz.
And Fly Guy said— BUZZ!

It was time for lunch.
Buzz gave Fly Guy
something to eat.

Fly Guy was happy.

Chapter 3

Buzz took Fly Guy to
The Amazing Pet Show.

The judges laughed.
"Flies can't be pets," they said.
"Flies are pests!"

Buzz was sad.
He opened the jar.
"Shoo, Fly Guy," he said.
"Flies can't be pets."

But Fly Guy liked Buzz.
He had an idea.
He did some fancy flying.

The judges were amazed. "The fly can do tricks," they said. "But flies can't be pets."

Then Fly Guy said—

The judges were more amazed. "The fly knows the boy's name," they said. "But flies can't be pets."

Fly Guy flew high, high, high
into the sky!

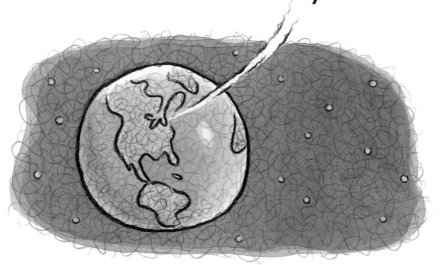

Then he dived down, down, down into the jar.

"The fly knows his jar!" the judges said. "This fly _is_ a pet!" So they let Fly Guy in the show.

TALLEST PET

PET WITH MOST LEGS

CUTEST PET

He even won an award.

And so began a
beautiful friendship.